CW00376336

© 1992 Carol Thompson
This edition published
in 1996 by Leopard Books,
a division of Random House UK Ltd,
20 Vauxhall Bridge Road,
London SW1V 2SA

First published in 1992 by Julia MacRae Books

ISBN 0 7529 0179 6

Printed in Singapore

My Counting Book

CAROL THOMPSON

LEOPARD

One heavy hippo

Two plump penguins

Three cuddly cats

Four tough teddy bears

Five zebras crossing

Six swimming pigs

Seven leaping frogs

Eight fat hens

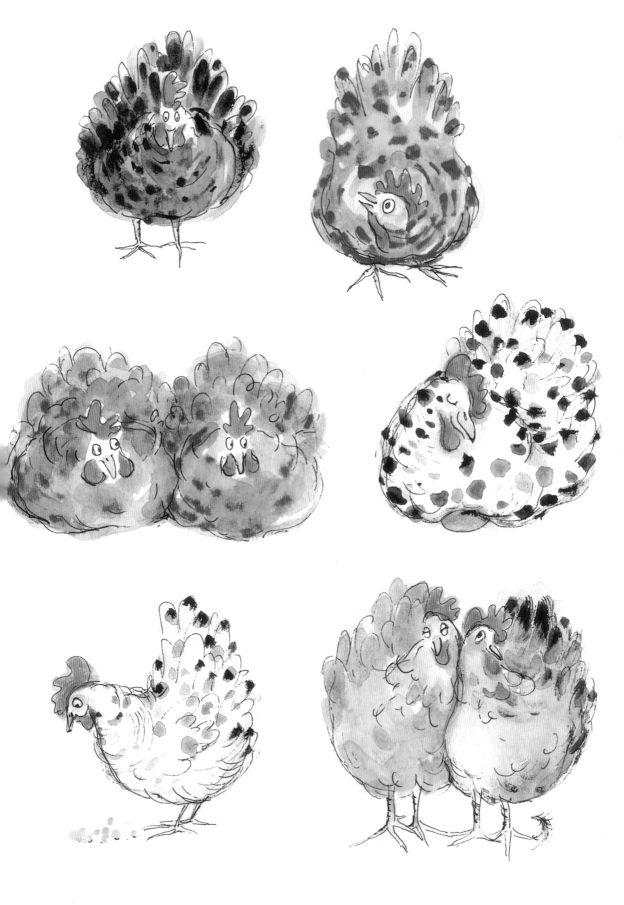

Nine nibbling rabbits

Ten peeping faces